Jeremy Bean's
St. Patrick's Day

This one's for John.
A. S.

For Kurt,
who, in second grade,
wore jeans that were not blue.
L. S.

Printed in Hong Kong.
First Edition 4 5 6 7 8 9 10 11 12 13
Library of Congress Cataloging in Publication Data
Schertle, Alice.   Jeremy Bean's St. Patrick's Day.
Summary: Shy Jeremy Bean forgets, much to his
humiliation, to wear green to school for St. Patrick's Day.
[1. St. Patrick's Day—Fiction. 2. Schools—Fiction]
I. Shute, Linda, ill.   II. Title. PZ7.S3442Je   1987
[Fic]   86-7403
ISBN 0-688-04813-7   ISBN 0-688-04814-5 (lib. bdg.)

Jeremy Bean's
St. Patrick's Day

BY Alice Schertle   ILLUSTRATED BY Linda Shute

Lothrop, Lee & Shepard Books   New York

J eremy Bean hummed a tune on his way to school.
Today would be a good day. Mrs. Cooperman's class
was going to plan the St. Patrick's Day party.
   Jeremy hurried across the playground, up the big
stone steps, and into the hall. There was Mr. Dudley,
the principal, standing in front of his office.

Jeremy Bean slowed down. Maybe today wasn't such a good day after all.

Jeremy wasn't exactly afraid of Mr. Dudley. It was just that the principal was so tall, and so bald, and had such a big brown mustache, and such a big, deep voice. Whenever Jeremy saw Mr. Dudley, he felt very small and very shy.

"Hi, there," said Mr. Dudley in his big, deep voice.

Jeremy looked down at his shoes. "Hi," he said, in a small voice.

"Happy Day-Before-St.-Patrick's-Day," said Mr. Dudley.

Jeremy Bean didn't know what to answer, so he just hurried down the hall and into his room.

That morning Mrs. Cooperman read her class a story about St. Patrick. Then everyone drew pictures of the kind man who lived in Ireland long ago. Jeremy gave him lots of gray hair and a long beard, but no mustache.

"Who knows the special St. Patrick's Day color?" asked Mrs. Cooperman.

"Green!" answered everyone at once.

"Green for the hills and valleys of Ireland and the shamrocks that grow there," said the teacher. "Let's think of some green food to eat at our St. Patrick's Day party tomorrow."

Jeremy's class decided to have green apples, celery, pickles, lime punch, and cupcakes with green icing at the party. And everyone would wear something green.

"I'm going to wear my Alligator Man T-shirt," said William.

"I'll ask if I can wear my mama's green necklace," said Louisa.

"I have green socks," said Jason. "I'll wear those. Everyone in the whole school will be wearing green tomorrow!"

"I'll wear my green sweater," said Jeremy Bean.

When Jeremy got home, he took his green sweater out of the closet. He tied the sweater around his waist and kicked the soccer ball around the backyard.

He rolled the sweater up and sat on it during supper. "Jeremy is growing taller," said his father.

He wore it as a cape when he played superhero until
bedtime.

He put it on over his pajamas.

In the middle of the night, Jeremy woke up. He was
too hot, so he took off the green sweater.

The next morning Jeremy got dressed and made his bed. When he was through, the bed had lots of lumps in it, just as it always did. One of the lumps was a little bigger than the others, but Jeremy didn't notice.

On the way to school, Jeremy smiled at Mr. Gillis, who was mowing his lawn.

"Happy St. Patrick's Day," called Mr. Gillis.

Jeremy stopped smiling.
He looked down at his clothes.
Yellow shirt, blue pants. No green.
Jeremy pulled up his pant legs.
Brown shoes, gray socks. *No green!*

He checked his underwear,
even though he knew he wasn't
wearing green underwear.

Louisa and William walked up.
"Oh-oh," said William. "Jeremy's not wearing green."
He and Louisa skipped off, singing,
>"Jeremy Bean,
>Didn't wear green!
>Jeremy Bean,
>Didn't wear green!"

Jeremy picked some leaves and stuck them
into his shirt pocket. Then he hurried after them.

In the schoolyard, Mary Ellen said,
"Where's your green, Jeremy?"
Jeremy showed her the leaves.
"Leaves don't count," said Jason.
"Jeremy Bean,
Didn't wear green,"
sang Mary Ellen.
Pretty soon everyone was singing,
"Jeremy Bean,
Didn't wear green!
Jeremy Bean,
Didn't wear green!"
"Stop it!" shouted Jeremy.

He ran into the school building. There was Mr. Dudley, standing in the hall, wearing a green bow tie, a green jacket, and a tall green hat. He was looking down at some papers in his hand.

Jeremy did not wait for Mr. Dudley to look up. He darted into a closet and closed the door.

The closet smelled of soap and paint and floor wax. Jeremy squeezed in between a mop and a push broom. Huddled in the dark, he wondered what Mr. Dudley would say to someone who forgot to wear green on St. Patrick's Day.

Then Jeremy heard footsteps.

The closet door opened slowly.

Mr. Dudley, the principal, looked down at Jeremy
Bean. "Will you please come into my office," he said.

Jeremy had never been in the principal's office before.
He stood in front of the big desk and waited.

He waited for Mr. Dudley to say, "Where is your green?"

He waited for Mr. Dudley to say, "Don't you know the
rules, Jeremy Bean?"

"You know, Jeremy," said Mr. Dudley, "sometimes I feel
like hiding in the broom closet myself."

"You do?" said Jeremy.

"Oh, yes," said the principal. "Especially when I have so much work to do. Look at all these papers on my desk. Do you think you could help me?"

Jeremy helped Mr. Dudley with the papers. He stacked some of them into neat piles. He stapled some of them together.

"You're a good helper," said Mr. Dudley. He didn't ask why Jeremy was not wearing green. He didn't even ask what Jeremy had been doing in the broom closet.

They talked about soccer, and square dancing, and their favorite TV programs.

After a while, Jeremy said, "I forgot my green sweater this morning. Everybody was teasing me."

"Well," said Mr. Dudley, "as you can see, I'm wearing plenty of green. I think I can spare some."

He put his hat on Jeremy's head.

But it wasn't quite right.

He let Jeremy try on his jacket.

But that wasn't quite right either.

Then Mr. Dudley tied his green bow tie
around Jeremy's neck. And it was perfect.

Jeremy looked up at the very big smile under Mr. Dudley's very big mustache. "Mr. Dudley," he said, "would you like to come to our St. Patrick's Day party?"

"I'd be delighted," said Mr. Dudley in his nice, deep voice.

Jeremy and the principal walked to class together.

"My friend Jeremy Bean invited me to the party," said Mr. Dudley.

"My friend Mr. Dudley lent me his bow tie," said Jeremy Bean.

They sat down and helped themselves to celery, green
apples, pickles, lime punch, and cupcakes with green icing.

DATE DUE			